Football Queen

by Marci Peschke

illustrated by Tuesday Mourning

PICTURE WINDOW BOOKS

a capstone imprint

Kylie Jean is published by Picture Window Books
A Capstone Imprint
1710 Roe Crest Drive
North Mankato, Minnesota 56003
www.capstonepub.com

Library of Congress Cataloging-in-Publication Data

Peschke, M. (Marci)

Football queen / by Marci Peschke ; illustrated by Tuesday Mourning.

p. cm. -- (Kylie Jean)

Summary: Kylie Jean Carter has been waiting for three years to become a Little
Dazzler—a junior cheerleader for the high school's Dancing Dazzlers—so she can
cheer for her brother's high school football team.

ISBN 978-1-4048-6799-4 (library binding) -- ISBN 978-1-4048-7210-3 (pbk.)

1. Cheerleading--Juvenile fiction. 2. School sports--Juvenile fiction. 3. Football
stories. 4. Brothers and sisters--Juvenile fiction. 5. Texas--Juvenile fiction. [1.
Cheerleading--Fiction. 2. Football--Fiction. 3. Brothers and sisters. 4. Texas--Fiction.]
I. Mourning, Tuesday, ill. II. Title.

PZ7.P441245Fo 2012

813.6--dc23   2011029704

Creative Director: Heather Kindseth
Graphic Designer: Emily Harris
Editor: Beth Brezenoff
Production Specialist: Danielle Ceminsky

Design Element Credit:
Shutterstock/blue67design

Printed in the United States of America in Stevens Point, Wisconsin.
072012
006833R

For Tina
with love for Rick
—MP

Table of Contents

All About Me, Kylie Jean!

My name is Kylie Jean Carter. I live in a big, sunny, yellow house on Peachtree Lane in Jacksonville, Texas with Momma, Daddy, and my two brothers, T.J. and Ugly Brother.

T.J. is my older brother, and Ugly Brother is . . . well . . . he's really a dog. Don't you go telling him he is a dog. Okay? I mean it. He thinks he is a real true person.

He is a black-and-white bulldog. His front looks like his back, all smashed in. His face is all droopy like he's sad, but he's not.

His two front teeth stick out, and his tongue hangs down. (Now you know why his name is Ugly Brother.)

Everyone I love to the moon and back lives in Jacksonville. Nanny, Pa, Granny, Pappy, my aunts, my uncles, and my cousins all live here. I'm extra lucky, because I can see all of them any time I want to!

My momma says I'm pretty. She says I have eyes as blue as the summer sky and a smile as sweet as an angel. (Momma says pretty is as pretty does. That means being nice to the old folks, taking care of little animals, and respecting my momma and daddy.)

But I'm pretty on the outside and on the inside. My hair is long, brown, and curly.

I wear it in a ponytail sometimes, but my absolute most favorite is when Momma pulls it back in a princess style on special days.

I just gave you a little hint about my big dream. Ever since I was a bitty baby I have wanted to be an honest-to-goodness beauty queen. I even know the wave. It's side to side, nice and slow, with a dazzling smile. I practice all the time, because everybody knows beauty queens need to have a perfect wave.

I'm Kylie Jean, and I'm going to be a beauty queen. Just you wait and see!

Chapter One
Dazzler Dynamo

Today still feels like summer. But as I sit in Momma's van, waiting for her to bring me to Little Dazzler camp, I look down Peachtree Lane. And what do I see but trees covered with leaves that look like cherry, lemon, and orange Jolly Rancher candies.

The colorful leaves swirl around, tumbling across our driveway. While I wait, I count them. One, two, three . . .

When I get to thirteen, I stop. I sure wish my momma would hurry up.

I open the van door and holler, "Momma, we're fixin' to be late for my Little Dazzler camp. Are you comin'?"

Momma comes out the door and locks up. "You just hold your horses, Little Miss," she says. "I'll get you to the high school on time, I promise."

She opens the back door and tosses her purse on the backseat. Then she hops in the driver's seat. We both buckle our seat belts.

"Ready?" she asks.

"Yes, ma'am, I sure am!" I say. "I can't wait to be a Little Dazzler!"

Every year, each girl on the high school drill team, the Dancing Dazzlers, can choose a younger girl to be their buddy at Little Dazzler Camp.

My big cousin Lilly isn't on the team, so I had to have a different girl pick me.

Grace Bryan chose me. Miss Clarabelle lives on one side of me, and on the other side is where Grace lives. She's a drill team girl, and I think T.J. is sweet on her. (That means he wishes she would be his girlfriend.)

When Grace picked me, she made me happier than a twirler with two batons. I bounce around in my seat, just thinking about it.

Momma smiles. "You seem excited," she says.

I nod happily. After all, I've been waiting for three years to be a Little Dazzler. I'm finally old enough to get picked. I tell Momma, "Grace is the best neighbor in the whole wide world! After Miss Clarabelle, I mean."

Momma nods. "We are very lucky to have Grace for our neighbor. You be sure to do your best today so she'll be proud she picked you."

"I will, Momma. Doing my best is my specialty," I reply. "Do some folks do their worst?"

The van stops at a red light and Momma turns around in her seat. She looks me straight in the eye. This means we are going to have a serious talk.

Momma says, "Most folks do the best they can, but if they don't try at all, then that is a bad thing. We Carters are never quitters. We try our best."

I look Momma right back in the eye. Then I nod. "Quitting is not for Carters or beauty queens," I say.

The streetlight flashes green. Momma turns and starts driving again. Soon, we turn into the Jacksonville High School parking lot.

Grace is waiting by her daddy's orange pickup truck. He also has an orange flag with horns on it in front of his house. Orange is his college color. He's a Texas Longhorn, and he wants Grace to be one when she goes to college, too.

Grace sees us and smiles. She waves at me, and I wave back.

Grace is tall and
has soft brown eyes.
Today, her curly red
hair is pulled into a
ponytail. She's wearing
black shorts and a pink
striped shirt.

Momma rolls
down the window as
we pull up. She says,
"Grace, you sure are a
sweet girl to pick Kylie
Jean for Little Dazzler
Camp. She has so
much energy. I think
she'll be a Dazzler
dynamo, don't you?"

Grace replies, "Yes, ma'am, she sure will. And you know, I wouldn't want to pick anyone else. Kylie Jean has had her heart set on this for quite a while!"

Momma laughs. "We have been talking about Little Dazzler Camp for years!"

I hop out of the car. "I love your shirt," I tell Grace.

Grace smiles. "Pink is my color," she says.

I gasp. "Mine too!" I say.

Grace reaches for my hand and we wave goodbye to Momma. After Momma drives away, Grace asks, "Before we get to the football field to practice, do you have any questions?"

"Is there a Dazzler queen?" I ask.

She frowns. "Hmm. Not exactly. We do have a drill team leader, though."

"Really?" I say. "Cool!"

We head to the field. Lots of big girls and little girls are there, standing side by side in pairs. Grace points to a woman with a whistle around her neck and says, "That's Coach Fowler."

The coach blows her whistle and we all sit down on the grass to listen.

She explains that the Little Dazzlers will only practice for an hour every Saturday morning. Then the big girls on the real drill team, like Grace and Maggie Lou, will have to stay for the whole morning.

All of us little girls, like Susie and me, will learn a dance routine, and then we will get to perform at one halftime show during the football season. A few of us will get picked for each game until every Little Dazzler gets a chance to perform.

Excitement bubbles up inside me like soda pop fizz. When the coach blows her whistle again, we all line up and watch the big girls go through their dance routine.

They are awesome! When they're done, I shout, clap, and jump up and down.

Grace laughs. "Hey, you're not at cheerleading camp, cutie!" she says. "It's time to dance!" So we do!

Chapter Two
Friday Night Football

My family, my town, and pretty much everyone in Texas spends the week getting ready for Friday night football. This year is especially exciting because my brother is the QB. That means quarterback.

Oh—I better say that it's T.J., not Ugly Brother, who is playing for the undefeated Jacksonville Kings football team. Ugly Brother could really take a bite out of those players on the other teams, but it just wouldn't be fair if we got a bulldog to play for us and they didn't.

Every day after school, T.J. has to go practice with Coach Armstrong and his team. He's number 13. Some people think that's an unlucky number, but I know it's a good number for my brother!

Momma goes to watch and sometimes takes me along. We sit on the sidelines while Momma cheers for all the boys on the team.

I cheer extra loud for T.J.

In Texas, even in the fall, it is pretty hot right after school, and I feel sorry for those poor football boys running and practicing football plays under the pounding sun.

But football makes them big stars. All over the state, TV news stations show stories about high school teams, star players, pep rallies and halftime performances.

On Wednesday night, we are eating tacos. Daddy picked up our food from Taco Casa on his way home from work. We all gather around the table and fill our plates from the brown paper sacks.

Mmmmm . . . smells like spicy taco heaven! I love Taco Casa!

When everybody has their food, Daddy asks, "How's practice going, son?"

T.J. looks at Momma and says, "I play better when Momma comes to watch."

Momma smiles. "T.J. Carter, that is one of the sweetest things I've ever heard!" she says. She turns to Daddy and adds, "Those boys on the team are working so hard. The Kings just have to have a winning season. We're going all the way to the state championships, I just know it!"

Daddy grins. "Well, wouldn't that be something!" he says. "The last time we went all the way to state, I was on the team."

"But you played defense, right, Daddy?" I ask.

"That's right," Daddy says.

Then T.J. says, "I know we can get to the championship if Kylie Jean comes to all the games. She's my secret good luck charm."

I can't believe it!

Me? My big brother's good luck charm? My mouth drops open and I jump out of my chair, shouting, "Really, me? For real? I'm your good luck charm? Me?"

T.J. grins. "Yup! I need all that energy cheering for me," he says. "Then I can play like an NFL pro."

"I'm your number-one fan, big brother!" I say.

Ugly Brother barks under the table. I can't tell if he wants to be a fan, too, or if he just wants to eat some of my taco.

Before I can figure it out, Momma warns, "T.J. and Kylie Jean, you better quit talking and start eating! You both have homework to do."

We both say, "Yes, ma'am."

* * *

That night, when I get in my big pink fluffy bed, Ugly Brother gets comfy at the end of the bed.

First he lies down on his side, then he stretches out long, and finally he gets on his stomach. This means he's going to snore.

He is a good brother, even if he sounds like a pig grunting when he gets to snoring loud.

We both settle down. He gets back on his stomach. I pull the covers right up to my nose so I'm nice and warm.

My body is as still as a statue, but my mind is racing like a horse.

I am thinking about how lucky I am to be a Little Dazzler. I wonder who will get to dance at the homecoming game.

Tomorrow is Thursday, which means we only have one more day until Friday night football. On Friday, they will have a big pep rally at the high school, and Lilly will cheer.

Maybe someday I could be a cheerleader, too.

The game is an away game, which means our team has to go to another town to play football. I can hardly wait.

I love football! That's what makes me such an awesome fan.

Besides, if I didn't like football, well, I just couldn't be a Texan anymore. I'd have to go live somewhere else. Good thing that'll never happen!

Chapter Three
Away Game

On Friday evening, Momma and I bring T.J. to the high school. There are three big yellow buses that say Jacksonville High School on the sides waiting to take the team, the cheerleaders, and the band over to Athens for the game.

T.J. looks like a giant in his purple football pants and white jersey with a big gold 13 on the front. He has his helmet in his hand.

Our cousin Lilly pokes her head out of a bus window and shouts, "Hey, Aunt Shelly, Kylie Jean, and T.J."

Momma hollers, "Lilly, you better cheer extra loud tonight since it's an away game."

Lilly gives us a thumbs up. Then I see that Grace is on the bus, too. She waves at me and I wave back, nice and slow, side to side. That's my special beauty queen wave. T.J. grabs his duffle bag, ready to get on the bus.

Momma grabs his hand. "You're going to lead your team to victory," she says. "Just play from the heart and remember everything Coach Armstrong taught you. Don't forget to drink lots of water, too."

T.J. smiles. "Yes, ma'am!" he says.

"Don't worry," I tell my big brother. "I'll be cheering for you so you can win."

He says, "Lil' Bit, I knew I could count on you. You're my good luck charm."

T.J. gives us one last wave as he climbs onto the bus. Momma, Daddy, and I will all ride to Athens in the van. We can't leave until Daddy gets home from work.

When we get home, Momma gets busy changing into her Kings T-shirt. I notice Ugly Brother didn't even eat a bite of the food in his dish.

I say, "We're going to eat on the road. Probably we'll have hamburgers."

Ugly Brother whines.

I ask, "Are you sad because you can't eat hamburgers?"

He barks, "Ruff."

Two barks mean yes. One means no. So what's wrong?

Suddenly an idea hits my brain like a tackle on a quarterback. I say, "You're sad because you're going to miss T.J.'s game! Right?"

He barks excitedly, "Ruff, ruff."

I come up with a plan. "Okay," I say. "Eat fast. Then I'll hide you in the van. I hope Momma and Daddy won't be too mad. I know it would break your heart to miss T.J.'s game."

I figure we'll need his doggie leash and he'll have to have something to wear that will show his school spirit. I have just the thing! I run upstairs to grab some purple and gold hair ribbons.

Back downstairs, I tie the ribbons in a big bow around his neck. Then we slip outside.

Carefully, I slide open the side door to the van. Ugly Brother tries to jump up, but he's so fat he needs a boost.

"You might need to go on a doggie diet," I tell him.

Ugly Brother growls at me. Whispering, I warn him, "You have to be quiet for our plan to work."

He climbs all the way into the back of the van and I throw an old blanket over him.

Daddy pulls up in his truck just as I close the van's door. He sees me standing by the van and says, "Hey, sugar. Where's your momma? I see you're all ready to go."

I say, "Yes, sir. I think I'll wait right here in the van. Momma's inside getting ready." As soon as he goes inside, I let out a big sigh of relief.

Before you know it, Momma and Daddy dash out and hop into the van.

On our way out of town, we get our burgers. Then we head on down the road on Highway 175, winding our way over the back roads. Ugly Brother does pretty good, but after a while, the smell of those burgers finally gets to him and he starts to whine.

Momma asks, "Did you hear that?"

I say, "Hear what?"

Daddy looks at Momma. "I did hear something," he says. "It sounded like a dog."

I decide I better confess. I blurt out, "Ugly Brother is back here with me. I just couldn't leave him home all alone! He was so sad that we were all going to the game without him, so I decided to help him out. Please don't be mad. Okay?"

Daddy laughs, but Momma is not happy. I can tell because she uses all of my names. "Kylie Jean Carter, I can't believe you brought Ugly Brother and didn't ask me if it was okay first!" she says.

"He was so sad," I say. "His heart was breaking right in two!"

Momma still looks mad, but she says, "It's too late to take him back now, so I hope he'll be a good fan at the game."

"He will be," I say. "I promise!"

And from underneath his blanket, Ugly Brother barks, "Ruff, ruff!"

When we get to the Athens High School stadium, we climb up thirteen steps to find enough room for all of us to sit.

It takes a long time to get to a seat because everyone wants to stop us and ask about Ugly Brother. They ask us his name, if he's a Kings fan, and how long has he been coming to football games. One man says Ugly Brother is a very unusual football fan. One lady comments on his school spirit because he is wearing a purple and gold bow.

The crowds love Ugly Brother, but they love T.J. more. We get so excited watching him play that I shout and Ugly Brother sits up and howls. I wave my purple foam finger in the air, jumping up and down.

The game is not even close. We have a huge lead and one more chance to score in the last few minutes of the fourth quarter.

T.J. has the ball. Daddy yells, "You got it, son! Take your time. Now pass the ball, pass the ball!"

T.J. looks around to see who is open. He throws the ball in a long, long arc down the field and into the hands of Junior Watts, who carries it over the line.

Another touchdown! The stands go crazy!

We are all yelling and hugging and smiling and happy. The players from the other team line up to shake hands with our team and say congratulations. The boys on our team look real proud.

Momma and Daddy and Ugly Brother and I push through the crowd like little fish against the tide. Everyone is leaving, but we are trying to get to T.J.

When he sees us, he comes to the sidelines. Momma gives him a hug and Daddy shakes his hand.

Momma says, "You are a superstar, T.J. Carter!"

Daddy adds, "Son, you've got the moves. That last pass was perfect!"

T.J. sees Ugly Brother and me standing there grinning, and he smiles. "Looks like I've got a new fan tonight," he says.

I laugh. "He really loves football," I explain, "and he hates being left behind."

Momma gives me a look so I know she isn't over being mad at me yet. I look at T.J. and admit, "I'm kind of in trouble for sneaking him into the van."

T.J. says, "I don't think good luck charms should get in trouble!" Then a bunch of other players come by and drag him away. He waves in our direction as they head for the locker room. The team will go to the Little Italy Pizza Parlor to celebrate and T.J. will get home late.

Momma, Daddy, Ugly Brother, and I head to the van. We have a long drive ahead of us. Momma and Daddy's whispering sounds like a lullaby and the road rocks me to sleep, so the next thing I know, Daddy is carrying me up to my bed. I have football dreams all night long.

Chapter Four

Thirteen Moves

The next day is Saturday. When I wake up, my eyes feel glued shut, I'm so tired. Rubbing the sleep out of my eyes, I look at my little pink tick-tock clock. It says 8:45.

Oh, no! I'm going to be late for Dazzler practice!

Now I have to hurry to get ready. I throw on my dance clothes and try to smash down my wild hair. But when I look in the mirror, I decide I better get Momma to brush my hair into a ponytail.

I shout, "Momma! Momma! I'm late for Little Dazzlers."

"Come on down so I can fix your hair," Momma calls.

It's funny how mommas know things. I didn't even have to ask her to fix my hair. She already knew I had crazy hair.

When I get to the kitchen, she's waiting with a brush, a hair band, Pop-Tarts, and a juice box.

"Daddy and Ugly Brother are taking you to Little Dazzlers today," Momma tells me, sitting me down on a stool and handing me a Pop-Tart. "Daddy has been so busy washing his truck he forgot to wake you up while I was out back raking leaves."

She brushes the hair on the sides and top of my head, slipping it all into the pink hair band. Then she turns me around to see how I look. "You'll do," Momma says. "Be good and mind Grace. You hear me?"

I hop off the stool. Hurrying toward the back door, I say, "I will, Momma."

Out in the driveway, the truck looks brand new! I give a long, low-down whistle. Daddy says, "Thank you, Sugar Pie. We better get going. You're going to be late, and it's my fault!"

Ugly Brother is already sitting in the front seat waiting for us. We jump in and take off. Riding in a truck makes you feel like you're on top of the world. I gobble down my Pop-Tarts and slurp up my juice.

In ten minutes, we're pulling up to the field. I give Daddy a kiss. He says, "Bye, Little Dazzler. See you in an hour."

I find Grace right away. First things first, Coach teaches us a routine that has thirteen steps. We all step up, then step back, turn around, snap your fingers, clap your hands out in front, behind your back, over your head, roll your body like a wave, jump, two steps left, and one step right. Grace and I go over the dance moves nice and slow. Grace is a good teacher.

"You've got rhythm," Grace tells me. "That's a good thing. All we have to do is learn our steps! You just keep your eyes on me and do what I do. Okay?"

"I'm gonna be your shadow," I say.

When Grace moves, I move. My eyes are glued to her like lace on a valentine. The coach walks around, making sure everyone is doing the dance right. When I see her coming, I smile real big and try to do everything just perfect! I want to do a real good job so she'll pick me to dance at the next game.

"You two are doing great," Coach says. "You think you could help Maggie Lou and Susie? They're having some trouble."

"Sure thing," Grace says.

My friend Susie and her high-school dancer Maggie Lou come over to us. Susie says, "You gotta help me, Kylie Jean! I can't do all these moves!"

I say, "Just keep your eyes on me and do what I do, okay?"

Before long, we are both dancing our hearts out. We don't even have to think of the steps anymore, we just know them. Grace is helping Maggie Lou, too. The four of us line up and take it from the top. We do the whole dance routine, no mistakes, and then Coach blows the whistle. I can't believe it. It's already time to go!

Susie moans. "I don't want to go yet," she says. "I was just starting to have fun!"

Maggie Lou says, "Don't be sad. I'll see you next week. Okay?"

"We can practice during our recess this week if you want to," I tell Susie.

That makes her smile. "Great idea," she says. Then she sees her mom. "Gotta go. See you at school!"

Daddy honks his horn. No one could miss seeing his super clean shiny truck. I wave and pick up my practice bag. Walking across the field to the truck, I hear loud music behind me. The older girls are starting to learn another routine.

When I climb up into the truck, Daddy gives me a high five. He says, "Sugar Pie, you were awesome! I saw you helping your friend, too. Great job!"

Ugly Brother barks, "Ruff, ruff!"

"See?" Daddy says. "Ugly Brother thinks so, too. Say, how about a Slush Puppy slushy from the Drive-N-Go?"

I say, "Yay!" Then I scoot across the seat to give him a big squeezy hug.

Daddy laughs and says, "If you're gonna give me a big hug every time we go get a slushy, I guess we'll go more often!"

"How about every day?" I suggest.

Daddy says, "Hugs for sure. If you drink a grape slushy every day, you'll turn into a giant grape!"

I cross my arms. "Daddy, I will not turn into a grape!" I say. "Don't worry, though, I'll still give you hugs anyway."

Daddy looks relieved. "Good. I sure do love those hugs!" he tells me. Soon he pulls into the Drive-N-Go. It's busy, so I wait in the truck. Saturdays are always real busy around our town. I guess people just like to get out on Saturdays to do all the things they like to do.

Daddy comes back with a grape slushy for me, a cherry one for Ugly Brother, and a mixed one for him. My grape slushy is cold and sweet and delicious. "Thanks, Daddy," I say.

"You earned it," Daddy says. "You were real nice to your friend, and you tried hard."

When we get home, I practice some more. I want to be the best Little Dazzler I can be.

Chapter Five
Biggest Fan Contest

Susie and I practice our dance steps all week long at recess. But all anyone can talk about is the big game coming up on Friday.

When Friday finally comes, I know the whole town is going to show their team spirit. There is a huge pep rally at the high school on Friday afternoon and everyone is invited.

I decide to wear my purple Kings Rule T-shirt. When we get to the high school gym, it seems like the whole town is there for the rally! I see lots of folks I know.

Everyone wants to show their school spirit and support the Kings. The gym is very loud, with all those people packed in there, but that's okay. After all, pep rallies are supposed to be loud!

I look around the room until I see my cousin Lilly. She and the other cheerleaders are standing on the basketball court. She waves at me and Momma. Then the cheerleaders start calling out cheers.

They chant, "Go purple!"

We yell back, "Go purple!"

They chant, "Go gold!"

We yell back, "Go gold!"

Everyone shouts, "Go Kings, all right, let's win tonight!"

The cheerleaders shake their gold and purple pom-poms. Then the school's band plays music and the drum line plays, too. They are the most fun to watch because they dance while they beat the drums.

Then the football team coach goes down to the floor. He shouts, "Here are your undefeated Kings!"

All of the players run out and I see T.J. The folks are stomping their feet in the stands and it sounds like thunder. Boom, boom, boom!

T.J. waves at Momma and me. I stand up and cheer extra loud.

The cheerleaders do another cheer. First, they make a pyramid with all the girls stacked up in a triangle.

Then they do a tricky stunt. Two girls throw Lilly up high. I hold my breath and then they catch her. Whew! I'd be scared if I were her, but she just keeps on smiling!

Everyone is excited and cheering and yelling and smiling. Then Lilly grabs the microphone. "You're going to want to hear this," she yells over the crowd. She waits until we get quiet. Then she goes on, "We're having a Biggest Fan contest. Some judges will be in the stands during the homecoming game looking for the biggest Kings  fans. The loudest, craziest, most loyal fans will be invited down to the field for the halftime show. Go ahead and get crazy, Kings fans!"

The folks in the stands go wild!

Lilly shouts, "Thanks for coming out! See y'all tonight at the game!"

Momma grabs my hand and pulls me toward the gym doors. In a few hours, T.J. will be playing against the Tyler Tigers. The Kings are going to win. I just know it!

Chapter Six
Home Game

At seven o'clock, it's finally game time! Our whole family is in the front row of the Jacksonville High School stadium. The stands are packed. The Tigers' fans are on the other side of the stadium. In our row, it's Granny, Pappy, Nanny, Pa, aunts, uncles, my best cousin Lucy, Momma, Daddy, me—even Ugly Brother is there!

On the field, all of the cheerleaders are cheering and dancing. When the players come out on the field, I jump up and down, waving my giant purple foam finger.

In the first quarter, T.J. throws a pass. Junior catches it! The Tigers defense pushes us back, though. At the end of the quarter, the score is 0-0. I've gotta get these fans going!

I shout, "Go purple, go gold, go Kings, go Carter!"

My family yells back, "Go purple, go gold, go Kings, go Carter!"

Soon the folks in stands join in. "Go purple, go gold, go Kings, go Carter!"

I clang my cowbell. They clang their cowbells. We just keep on clangin' and cheering.

In the second quarter, T.J. hands the ball to #44, Christian Harris. Daddy shouts, "Come on, Christian, you can do it!"

"Run, go, run!" I yell.

Christian runs all the way to the end zone. Touchdown! We all go wild, shouting and jumping and hugging.

Then our kicker steps up. He warms up, stretching for a minute. The fans hush. Just seconds ago, you couldn't hear a thing, and now it's so quiet I can hear a skeeter buzzing by me.

The kicker stands in front of the ball, takes three steps back, gets a running start, and then bam, he kicks it!

That ball slides though the goal posts just like a buttered biscuit.

I hug Lucy, Lucy hugs me, and we jump up and down together. I am so glad she's helping me cheer for T.J.

The score is now 7-0. The Kings are winning. It is halftime, and Ugly Brother and I are hungry for a snack.

"Daddy, can we please go to the concession stand and get some nachos?" I ask. "And can Lucy come, too?"

Daddy laughs. "Okay, Sugar Pie," he says. "But it's gonna be crowded. You two stay close."

I hold Daddy's hand, and Lucy holds my other hand. There are a lot of people trying to get a snack, and I get a little worried.

Since I'm T.J.'s good luck charm, I have to be back in the stands before the third quarter starts. Otherwise, who knows what could happen!

"How long is the line?" I ask Lucy.

She stands on her tiptoes, but she can't see the front of the line. "I don't know," she says. "But I think people are moving fast!"

Finally we get to the front of the line. Daddy orders cokes, nachos, a hamburger, and some curly fries.

I nudge Daddy and say, "Hey, don't forget to get Ugly Brother a hot dog!"

"Oh yeah, I almost forgot. A hot dog for the dog," Daddy adds, laughing. "Thanks for reminding me, Sugar Pie."

Lucy and I help him carry everything back. I'm carrying my nachos. "Mmmmm . . . I smell those spicy hot peppers," I say. My mouth is watering.

"Me too," Lucy says. "Yum!"

We make it back to our seats with plenty of time before the third quarter starts. Ugly Brother eats his hot dog in three big bites. Chomp, chomp, chomp.

Then he looks at my nachos.

"Don't you get any ideas," I say. "I'm already sharin' with Lucy, and hot nachos make you sick anyway. Remember?"

He barks, "Ruff, ruff." Then he whines a little, but the game starts, and I am too busy watching the third quarter to talk to him.

This game is getting good! On the sidelines, Coach Armstrong paces back and forth, following the action. The other team gets the ball. They get close enough to score a field goal, so the score is now 7-3.

I want to boo, but booing isn't nice even when you are trying to be the biggest fan. The other team has a good defense. Usually we have more points by now.

In the fourth quarter, T.J. throws a thirty-yard pass to Junior. Then Junior scores a touchdown with only a few seconds left in the game. In the stands, all of the Kings fans go crazy!

The Kings win, 14-3!

"He did it!" Daddy says, giving me a high five.

T.J. comes running over to us and gives me a sweaty hug. "You did it, good luck charm!" he whispers. Then he runs back to the rest of his team.

Chapter Seven
Dance or Cheer?

The very next day during Little Dazzler practice, Coach makes an announcement.

You won't believe what happened to Maggie Lou! Yesterday she sprained her ankle practicing at home when she accidently stepped in a gopher hole.

We are all shocked. Coach says, "I'm sorry to say she'll be out the rest of this season. Susie will have to dance with another Dazzler."

Right away, Susie starts to cry.

I pat her on the back and say, "Please don't cry! Everything will work out. Just you wait and see."

Susie hiccups. "Do you really think so?" she asks.

I give her a hug and say, "Yup!"

Then Coach has more to say. "I have the names of the Little Dazzlers who will be dancing during the homecoming halftime show," she says.

We all wait quietly. I have my fingers crossed. I'd cross my toes too if I could. Then an awful thought hits my brain like stink on a skunk.

I can't be a fan and a Little Dazzler.

Coach makes all the Dazzlers warm up under the bleachers during the second quarter. No exceptions!

Now I'm just hoping she doesn't say my name. If I get picked, I'll have to choose between being a fan and being a Little Dazzler.

She looks at her clipboard and announces, "Emily and Kylie Jean."

Grace gives me a high five and says, "Way to go, girl!"

I can't think of anything to say, and you know that is not normal for me. All my thoughts are swirling around in my brain.

You know I'm T.J.'s good luck charm and you also know Carters are not quitters.

Dancing with the Little Dazzlers is something I've wanted to do for a long, long time.

I don't know what to do.

Susie asks, "Are you okay? I thought you would jump around and scream or something. I would if I got picked to dance."

This makes me feel even worse! My friend doesn't even have a girl to dance with and she's worrying about me. "I'm okay," I say. "I just have to figure something out."

Just then, Coach blows her whistle. It's time to line up and practice our dance routine. We're even dancing with music today.

Susie just looks lost. She doesn't have Maggie Lou to dance with.

Then Grace says, "Hey, you can dance with us."

"That's a great idea!" I say.

But even when I'm dancing, I'm still feeling worried about my problem. It seems hard to breathe with all this worry on me.

When we take a break, I ask, "Grace, can I talk to you about something important?"

Grace looks concerned. "What's up?" she asks.

We sit down in the grass. "I'm T.J.'s good luck charm when he plays football," I begin. "If I'm not cheering in the stands, the team just might lose. It would be all my fault. Carters are not quitters, and neither are beauty queens, so I'm in a real pickle."

Grace frowns, like she's thinking. Then she asks, "So you don't want the team to lose, but you don't want to be a quitter?"

"Being a Little Dazzler has been my dream for a long time," I say. "It makes me real sad to think I wouldn't be there to dance with you after all you've done for me. But T.J. has a dream, too. He's been dreamin' of being a football star forever."

Grace smiles. "I think quitters stop because they can't do things or they're afraid they might not be any good at them. If you quit, I'll understand. You won't really be a quitter. You'll really just be choosing to give up one of your dreams to help your brother. Right?"

I think about it. "I never thought of it like that," I say.

Grace adds, "Besides, you won't be letting me down. You'll really be doing two good things at one time. Susie can dance with me, since Maggie Lou can't dance."

Suddenly I am able to breathe better and my mind is as easy as a spring day.

Momma always says if you put goodness out into the world, it will come back to you. Anyway, here I was all worried, and now I see I can help both T.J. and Susie.

Chapter Eight
Mums with Momma

After Little Dazzler practice, Momma and
I go to the craft store to buy supplies to make
homecoming mums. Homecoming mums are big
fancy corsages. I want my mum to be as big as
the moon, but I'll have to settle for one as big as a
dinner plate.

She asks, "Do you want purple or gold flowers?"

I answer, "Gold, please. They look like
sunshine."

Momma chooses purple for herself.

When I am old enough to go to high school, I will get two corsages: a fancy one made of real flowers for the homecoming dance and a big fun one like we're making now for the football game.

Who knows? I might even end up being the homecoming queen. You know how much being a queen means to me!

The most important thing about homecoming football mums is putting as many decorations on them as you can. My eyes spy some charms.

"Momma, just look at all these charms!" I say, pointing to the table. "They have every kind in the whole wide world."

Momma winks at me. "Not every kind, but they sure come close to having them all. How are you going to choose?"

My hands are just
itching to dip into the big
bowls of sparkly little silver and gold charms.
Momma hands me a little shopping basket.

"Go ahead and pick some charms out," she
tells me.

Right away I see a football and a football
helmet. Plop! They land in the bottom of the
basket. Next I see a cheerleader, pom-poms, and
a megaphone, which looks like a waffle cone with
the little end cut out so you can yell into it. After
that I see a football player and a goal post.

There's a big bowl of number and letter charms.
Digging around, I find the number 13 and the
letters T and J. Perfect! They go right into my
basket with the rest of the charms.

I see a whistle just like Coach Armstrong has and a #1. Those go in my basket too, of course.

Then I see the best charm. It's a tiny, perfect, little gold crown.

I gush, "Momma, look! I found the most perfect little gold crown and I just have to have it! We are the Kings, after all."

Momma laughs. "Leave it to you to find a crown in all of these charms," she says, looking at the bowls of charms. "There must be at least a couple hundred of them."

When I count them up, I have thirteen gold charms to glue on my mum. That's a lot!

I say, "Momma, I sure hope all these charms are going to fit!"

"Don't worry," she tells me. "You have a really big mum to put them on."

We buy yards and yards of yellow and purple ribbon. Miss Lonna, the craft store lady, measures it out and then cuts it. Snip, snip, snip. The colorful ribbons swirl in the bottom of my basket. Finally, we choose rows of sparkly gold letters to stick on the ribbons. The letters will spell out GO KINGS and T.J. CARTER and #13.

Miss Lonna rings everything up and loads it all into a huge bag.

I beg, "Can I please carry it to the van?" and Momma nods.

Miss Lonna says, "Thanks, and see you at the game."

At home, we spread everything out on the kitchen table. Then Momma gets her glue gun, and we get to work.

Momma is the queen of crafts, so I just let her do most everything. Sometimes she asks me where I want her to glue a charm.

Ugly Brother tries to help hold Momma's flowers. He doesn't try to eat them, but they turn his mouth purple!

When the mum is finally done, I sigh. "Momma, that is the biggest, prettiest, best football mum I've ever seen!" I tell her.

Then we hang it up to keep it safe until I wear it to the homecoming game on Friday night. If I'm going to be T.J.'s good luck charm and the best Kings fan in the stands, I need to have the prettiest flower ever!

Chapter Nine
A New Cheer

We only have one week until the homecoming game. That means I have five days to plan my fan costume and make up a new cheer. That's not a lot of time! I call Lucy. "Can you come over and help me make up a cheer for the big game?" I ask.

"You bet," Lucy says. "When do you want me to come over?"

I suggest, "After school tomorrow?"

"Sure, I'll ask my momma. If she says yes, I can ride home on the bus with you," she says.

After we both say goodbye, I go downstairs. In the kitchen, Momma is making plans for our tailgate party. Tailgate parties before the homecoming game are a Jacksonville tradition. They are kind of like a picnic in your pickup truck. You bring your lawn chairs and spread the food out on the tailgate.

Momma says, "I'm thinking about making pork barbeque for the tailgate party. What do you think?"

Licking my lips, I say, "Mmmm!"

Momma laughs. She puts pork roast on her list. "What else?" she asks.

I think for a second. Then I say, "I can make Granny's deviled eggs."

She says, "That's a great idea! I'll add eggs to my list."

"How about chocolate chip cookie bars?" I add.

Momma nods. "Perfect," she says. "I finally have the menu—pork barbeque, potato salad, chips, deviled eggs, and chocolate chip cookie bars. Sounds tasty, right?"

I say, "Yup!" and Ugly Brother barks, "Ruff, ruff!"

* * *

The next day after school, Lucy and I ride home together. We start to work on the cheer as soon as we get on the bus.

"I think the cheer should start with 'Kings are gonna rock you,'" I say.

Lucy says, "What rhymes with rock?"

"Clock, tock, and lock all rhyme," Susie says from behind us.

I write all those words in my notebook. "Thanks, Susie!" I say. All the way home to Peachtree Lane, Lucy and I play with words on paper, working on the cheer. We rhyme win, thin, tin, spin, pin, and fin. I write all the words down. Then we rhyme rule, school, fool, cool, and drool.

I say, "I think Ugly Brother would like it if we use drool. He is the king of doggie drool!"

Lucy is not so sure. "Drool is not cool, though," she says.

"Yeah, I guess you're right," I say. "Let's keep thinking."

We keep on thinking, rhyming, and writing. When we get to my house, Momma has a snack ready for us in the kitchen. Apple slices with caramel dip. We eat our snack and tell Momma all about our rhyming words.

I say, "The first line is, 'Kings are gonna rock you' and we are trying to rhyme the next line."

"But we're having trouble," Lucy says.

"Why don't you skip a line, and then rhyme the next line?" Momma suggests.

"I love that idea," I gush. "You are so creative, Momma!"

We add a line that says, "Kings are gonna sack you."

Now we go back to rhyme with rock and we choose clock. That fits just perfect! Lucy and I are real happy.

Then we choose a new word. We pick whack, but can't get it to sound right.

Finally we figure out that we need to put the word sack first and then use whack.

We are writing this cheer faster than chickens fry on the Fourth of July!

I scribble. I erase and add some more.

Finally we finish.

Then I read it out loud so Momma can hear, too.

Kings are gonna rock you
Kings are gonna sack you
Better watch the clock you
Our linebackers will whack you!
Kings are gonna win it
They throw the ball to spin it
Kings are gonna rule
Kings are really cool!
Go Kings, Go Kings!
Go Kings, Go Kings!

When I am done reading the cheer, I think to myself that it was pretty good. Maybe someday I should think about being a cheerleader!

Momma grins. "I like it. I really like it!"

Lucy says, "Yeah, we rocked it."

After Lilly stops by to pick up Lucy, I go upstairs to work on my #1 fan costume. I decide I will have to go all out. But what does a #1 fan and good luck charm wear?

I think of the NFL games I watch on TV with Daddy and remember that those fans wear paint. I'm going to need some paint for my face. I can paint one side purple and the other gold. I'll definitely need some ribbons in my hair and my Kings fan shirt.

I ask, "Ugly Brother, do you think I should change my pink shoelaces for purple?"

He barks, "Ruff, ruff."

I'll need something to carry all of my stuff, so I pack my huge purple foam finger, cowbells, pom-poms, and megaphone in my practice bag. When we go to the game, I will wear my giant football mum, too!

"Do you think I'll look like a real true #1 fan?" I ask Ugly Brother.

He barks, "Ruff, ruff."

Then he runs around the room because he is so excited. Now we are all ready, but we have to wait two more days for Friday night football!

Chapter Ten
Tailgate Party

There's a huge homecoming pep rally on Friday afternoon. Afterward, Momma and I go home and pack up our picnic.

When Daddy gets home, we will head over to the stadium parking lot in his truck. Granny and Pappy will meet us there, and Nanny and Pa will drive over in Pa's truck.

I can hardly wait. I am so full of excitement, I could do a touchdown dance!

Momma puts everything in Great-Granny's big picnic basket.

Then she says, "Kylie Jean, run up and get that red and white checkered cloth out of the closet upstairs."

I jump up the steps two at a time. Ugly Brother follows me, but he's a slowpoke. I am already starting to go back down when he gets to the top of the stairs.

The kitchen smells like chocolate cookies. Momma cuts the cookie bars and wraps them up.

"Can I have one now, please?" I beg.

Momma laughs, pointing at the pan. "We just happen to have one left. Let's split it," she says.

When Daddy comes in, we are just finishing our cookie bar. Momma gives him her last bite.

"You cook like an angel," he says. "That's delicious! Where's the rest?"

Momma tells him, "The rest are for later. You better hurry and get changed so we can get going."

Pulling his tie loose, Daddy heads for the stairs. Momma and I get everything stacked up by the back door. When Daddy comes back, he has on a Kings shirt, jeans, and tennis shoes.

He asks, "Are you two ready?"

That reminds me that I left my practice bag upstairs with my fan gear inside. I can't forget that!

"Almost ready!" I shout. "I have to get my bag." I scoot right upstairs to get it, and then out into Momma's van.

It doesn't take long to get to the high school. In our town, it doesn't take too long to get to just about any place you want to go.

Granny and Pappy are saving us a parking spot. Daddy backs into the parking spot and we let down the tailgate. Lucy, Nanny, and Pa are in the spot across from us. Lucy waves at me and I wave back at Lucy. I shout, "Come over here and eat with me!"

She yells, "Okay!"

We sit on the ground with Ugly Brother near the grown-ups. He has his own plate, and I'm glad, because if he didn't, he'd be after my plate.

Daddy, Pappy, and Pa are all talking about the game. Momma and Granny go over to talk to Nanny and the aunts.

Then Lucy and I see Susie and her family down by the end of the row.

I ask, "Daddy, can we go talk to Susie?"

He nods. "Take Ugly Brother and watch out for trucks coming in. Okay?"

Ugly Brother walks me, instead of me walking him. I try to pull back on the leash, but he smells hot dogs. I shout, "Slow down!" but he starts running. The only time he moves fast is when he is hungry.

Lucy chases after us. When Ugly Brother finally stops, we are at the end of the row of trucks.

Susie is there, laughing. She says, "Your dog is funny."

"More like hungry," I say.

Lucy asks, "Do you have hot dogs? He loves hot dogs."

"We sure do! Can he have one?" Susie asks me.

I consider. "He already ate, so maybe just one."

While Ugly Brother eats, we talk about the halftime show. Susie is ready! She asks, "Are you sure you don't want to dance?"

"No," I say, shaking my head. "I'm gonna be T.J.'s good luck charm and biggest fan tonight!"

I'm glad Grace helped me get out of my pickle. She's a good teacher and dancer. I think she's a good listener, too. I know I'm doing the right thing.

The sky starts turning a dusty blue-gray color, so we say goodbye and head back. It's almost game time, and everyone is packing up their picnics. The chairs and picnic baskets all go back in the trucks. Momma helps me paint my face. We get out our tickets and head for the gate.

It's time for me to cheer!

Chapter Eleven
The Big Game

The Kings are playing their rivals, the Groveton Gators. We all sit on the very first row of the center section. I like front row seats. Momma, Daddy, Ugly Brother, Granny, Pappy, Nanny, Pa, aunts, uncles, and Lucy all squeeze in close on the bench.

T.J. and Lilly are the only ones not in our row. That's because they're on the field.

Across from us, the stands are filled with Gators fans.

I ask Pa, "Do I look like a #1 fan?"

He laughs. "I like your mum. You are somethin' else. With everything you have on, you could be two fans!"

Nanny adds, "That mum is as big as a plate!"

Grinning, I say, "I know. Bigger is better when you're a good luck charm. T.J. needs to be able to see me from the field and I'm kind of short."

We look down at the players. It is green and white against purple and gold. I pull on my giant foam finger. Then I start to wave at the folks in the stands. The game is getting started!

In the first quarter, T.J. throws a pass and Junior Brown catches it. I get the folks in our row to do the wave when T.J. throws the ball. We stand up one by one and throw our arms in the air. Lots of people do it and it looks like there's a big wave rushing through the stands. The wave looks so good, I decide right then and there we're going to do it a lot!

The Gators stop the ball at the 50-yard line. Can you believe it? Those Gators have guts. They're a tough team. This is going to be harder than I thought! The score at the end of the first quarter is 0-0.

I run back and forth in front of the crowd, waving my giant purple foam finger and chanting, "Let's go, Kings!"

The crowd shouts back, "Let's go, Kings!" Then I rattle my cowbell.

Even with all my cheering, the Gators score a touchdown. The score at the end of the second quarter is 0-7. That means our boys need some help! I go all out to get the fans up in the stands! I lead them in a chant using my megaphone.

I call, "Who's the best?"

They shout, "The Jacksonville Kings are the best!"

T.J. throws another pass to #44. In the stands, we all do the wave.

This time he makes it to the end zone! We go wild! The game is tied 7-7! The Gators quarterback is good, but T.J. is better!

Now it's halftime. A lot of the Gators fans go to the concession stands, but I can't wait to see the show. It's awesome! Our cheerleaders make a pyramid and do some cheers that are new and exciting. Lilly gets tossed up and flies through the air lots of times and does some other new stunts.

Our band plays our school song. Then they march all over the field playing music, and when they stop they spell out K-I-N-G-S in giant letters.

The drum line performs a song that has us all up dancing in the stands.

Finally, the Dancing Dazzlers come out. I shout extra loud for Susie and Grace.

When the music starts, Susie does not miss one single step! I am so proud of her that I don't feel bad at all about not being on the field, not for one single minute.

Then the homecoming court comes out onto field. The queen looks so beautiful I think I might faint! Her crown sparkles likes the stars above us. Someday I'm going to be wearing that crown, I just know it!

After the homecoming queen has waved her way off the field, Lilly comes out. I get quiet and nervous.

Now Lilly is going to announce the winners of the Number One Fan contest. Lucy and I cross our fingers and toes and everything else.

Then Lilly says, "We have several super fans in the stands, but the #1 Kings fans are . . ." I don't hear any of the other names, because she says mine first! Kylie Jean Carter!

I run down to the field and T.J. meets me. He says, "Way to go, Lil' Bit! Keep on cheering. I need your help during the next half if we're going to win this." Then he swings me up on his shoulders and runs up and down the sidelines.

I know I'm supposed to be a #1 Kings fan right now, but I can't resist a little beauty queen wave, nice and slow, side to side, with my best dazzling smile!

The third quarter starts and it's really rough. Both teams are good.

I keep the Kings fans cheering, but the Kings do not score. The only good thing is the Gators don't score either! At the end of the third quarter, we are still tied 7-7.

After that, it looks like we're gonna end this game tied, but then the Gators make a field goal with only a few seconds left in the game! Ugly Brother whines. I am in shock. The score is 7-10. Oh, no! We just have to win! I have to do something!

"Go purple, go gold, go Kings, go Kings!" I scream.

My family yells back, "Go purple, go gold, go Kings, go Kings!"

Soon the folks in the stands join in. "Go purple, go gold, go Kings, go Kings!"

We stomp in the stands and it sounds like thunder. The Kings have to make a touchdown to win. Everyone stands up and we all join hands.

With five yards to go and ten seconds left in the game, Coach Armstrong runs a quarterback sneak. T.J. runs the ball into the end zone.

Touchdown! Kings win 14-10!

Daddy is shouting, "That's my boy!" and Momma is so excited she is crying. Lucy and I are jumping up and down and hugging.

Then I run all down the row slapping everyone's hand in a victory lap.

We won!

Every day, I dream about being a beauty queen. But right now, our whole town has big dreams of the state championships.

I have to keep on being a number-one fan and a good luck charm. With me in the stands and my big brother on the field, I just know we're going to win!

Marci Bales Peschke was born in Indiana, grew up in Florida, and now lives in Texas with her husband, two children, and a feisty black-and-white cat named Phoebe. She loves reading and watching movies.

When **Tuesday Mourning** was a little girl, she knew she wanted to be an artist when she grew up. Now, she is an illustrator who lives in South Pasadena, CA. She especially loves illustrating books for kids and teenagers. When she isn't illustrating, Tuesday loves spending time with her husband, who is an actor, and their two sons.

Glossary

corsage (kor-SAHJ)—a flower bouquet worn on clothing or a wrist

creative (kree-AY-tiv)—if you are creative, you use your imagination and are good at thinking of new ideas

dynamo (DY-nuh-moh)—a person who works very hard

halftime (HAF-time)—a short break in the middle of a game

megaphone (MEG-uh-fone)—a device shaped like a cone that is used to make the voice sound louder

pep rally (PEP RAL-ee)—a large meeting to boost cheer and spirit before an event

quarter (KWAR-tur)—one part of a game

rivals (RYE-vuhlz)—people you are competing against

routine (roo-TEEN)—a pattern of dance steps

tradition (truh-DISH-uhn)—the way things have been done

undefeated (uhn-di-FEET-id)—never beaten

Talk!

1. If you had to choose between cheering for T.J. and dancing with the Dazzlers, what would you choose? Why?

2. Kylie Jean's town gets excited about football. What do people at your school or in your town get excited about?

3. What do you think happens after this story ends?

Be Creative!

1. Kylie Jean's goal is to be a beauty queen. What's your number-one dream?

2. Who is your favorite character in this story? Draw a picture of that person. Then write a list of five things you know about them.

3. Draw a picture of a mum like Kylie Jean's. Then add charms that are important to you. What charms will you add? Why?

These cookies are great for cheering for your favorite team. Just make sure to ask a grown-up for help.

Love, Kylie Jean

CLASSIC FOOTBALL COOKIES

YOU NEED:
1 tube of sugar cookie dough (or box of cookie dough mix)
1 can of white frosting
Lots of different colors of food coloring (or choose your favorite team's colors)
A tube of white decorators' icing
A football-shaped cookie cutter
A grown-up helper

1. With your grown-up helper, roll out the cookie dough and cut football shapes with the cookie cutter. Bake as directed and let cool.

2. Divide the frosting into small bowls. Add food coloring to each bowl to create the perfect colors.

3. Frost cookies with colored frosting. Use the white decorators' frosting to add football laces. If you have other cookie cutters, you can get creative: try team jerseys, helmets, and pom-poms! Go team!

THE FUN DOESN'T STOP HERE!

Discover more at www.capstonekids.com

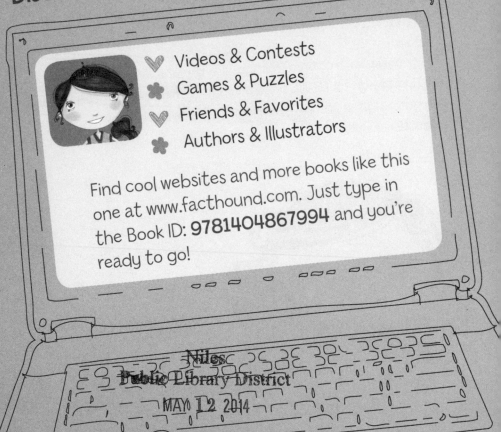

💜 Videos & Contests

✿ Games & Puzzles

💙 Friends & Favorites

✿ Authors & Illustrators

Find cool websites and more books like this one at www.facthound.com. Just type in the Book ID: **9781404867994** and you're ready to go!